• A FRANK ASCH BEAR BOOK •

SAND CAKE

• FRANK ASCH •

ALADDIN
New York London Toronto Sydney New Delhi

ALADDIN

For my dad

One summer day, the Bear family went to the beach, where they swam . . . and sunned themselves on a blanket.

After a while, Baby Bear said he felt like doing something else.

"If I make you a cake, will you eat it?" he asked Papa Bear.

"Sure," said Papa Bear. "If you use flour, milk, and eggs, I will be happy to eat your cake."

Baby Bear looked around. All
he could see was sand and water
for miles.

   "How can I find flour and
eggs and milk at the beach?"
asked Baby Bear.

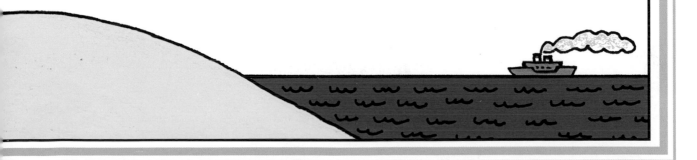

"That's easy," said Papa Bear.
"Eggs come from a chicken,

milk comes from a cow, and
flour comes from wheat."

"Well, if it is so easy," said Baby Bear, "then *you* make a cake with flour, milk, and eggs, and *I* will eat it."

"Okay," said Papa Bear, "I will," and he got up and went down to the water's edge. He picked up a stick that had washed up on the beach.

With the stick he drew a chicken in the wet sand. Under the chicken he drew an egg.

He scooped up the egg

and put it in Baby Bear's bucket.
   Then he drew some wheat
and ground it up in his hands to
make the flour. He added the
flour to the eggs.

Next, he drew a cow, and under the cow, a pail of milk. He poured the milk into the bucket with the eggs and flour.

On all of this he sprinkled some salt from the sea.

Then Papa Bear drew an oven.
Where the oven door was, he
dug a hole and buried the bucket.

"Come on," he said to Baby Bear, "let's go for a swim. By the time we come back, the cake will be ready for you to eat."

All the time Baby Bear
was swimming, he kept
wondering, "How will I ever
be able to eat that cake?"

When they came out of the water,
Papa Bear dug up the bucket . . .

and turned it upside down on the
beach. The cake was done.

"Well, now," said Papa Bear, "are you going to eat the nice cake I made for you?"

"Sure," said Baby Bear.

He picked up a stick and drew a picture of himself around the cake.

"Here I am, and I have eaten the cake. See it in my stomach?"

Papa Bear laughed and gave
Baby Bear a great big hug.
"Now I am hungry, too," he
said.

"Then you can both have some of
my cake," said Mama Bear, and she
opened the picnic basket. "I made
mine with *real* flour, milk, and eggs."
And it was delicious!